MISCHIEF IN THE FOREST

a Yarn Yarn

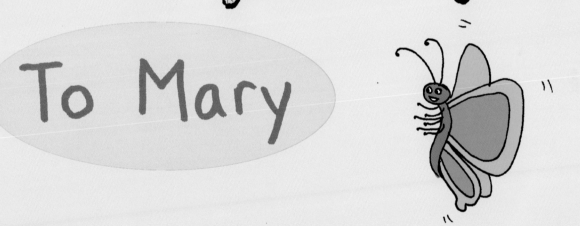

To Mary

by Derrick Jensen

pictures by Stephanie McMillan

Cover and interior design by Stephanie McMillan

LCCN: 2009912457
ISBN: 978-1-60486-081-8

Flashpoint Press
PO Box 903
Crescent City, CA 95531
www.flashpointpress.com

PM Press
PO Box 23912
Oakland, CA 94623
www.pmpress.org

10 9 8 7 6 5 4 3 2 1

Grandma Johnson was happy.

She was happy living alone
in her house in the forest.

She was happy having no neighbors.

She was happy sitting alone in
her living room knitting sweaters
for her grandchildren.

She was happy walking alone to and from the shed where she stored her yarn.

But there was a problem.

Sometimes she felt just a little bit lonely.
Not so much that she wasn't happy.
But just a little bit.

And so she was very happy as she got ready to go visit her grandchildren, who lived in the city.

She carried her suitcases
full of sweaters and mittens.

She was gone for a long time.
She had so much fun!

But she was happy to come
back to her house in the forest.

Only now she had two problems. One was that she would once again be just a little bit lonely.

The other was that SOMEONE
had been in her shed!

Who took her yarn? She couldn't
imagine. She lived all by herself,
and she had no neighbors.

She went to bed a little bit confused.

The next morning, she couldn't believe what she saw.

Her yarn!
The mystery was solved.

She had never seen anything so beautiful.

She followed the colorful
strands into the forest.

Although she had lived here for
years, she had never really
seen the forest before.

She wasn't alone at all!

She had neighbors.
Lots of neighbors!

They were as curious about her
as she was about them.

They were all so friendly.

She moved her rocking
chair outside, so she could
be closer to them.

And she kept her house open,
so they could be closer to her.

Her grandchildren came to visit.

They stayed for a while.
They got to know the neighbors.

But then they had to go
home to the city. "We'll be
back soon," they said.

They were sad to say goodbye.

They returned to the city, eager to
learn who their neighbors were there.

Now Grandma Johnson is happy.

She is happy living in
her home in the forest.

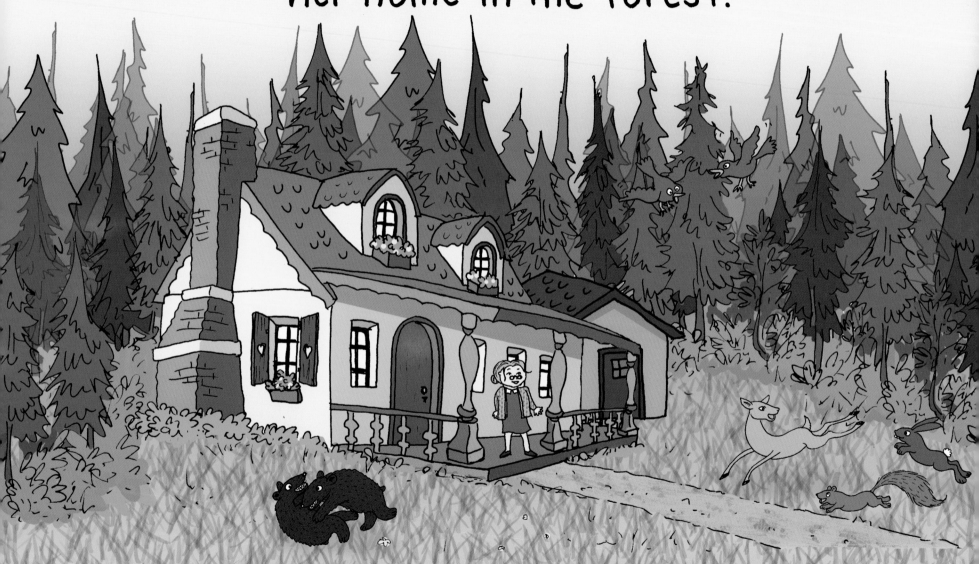

She is happy having neighbors.

She is happy sitting on her porch
knitting sweaters for her grandchildren.

She is happy walking to and from
her shed where she keeps her yarn.

And the happiest part of all for Grandma Johnson is that now she never feels lonely.

Not even the tiniest bit.

THE END

Many thanks to:
Wallace Global Fund

Aberbach
Scot Allen
Eric Cannizzaro
Steven L. Cloud
Virginia Evans
Rick Goheen
Laura E. (Ginsparg) Jones
David E. Lall
The Landau Family

Diane Leigh
Ivor MacKay
Chiji Ochiagha
Seth Al Paine
Tammy J. Parker
Ted Rall
Rico
Wil 'Doc' Schaefer
Stefan Wrangle

Derrick's neighbors include bears, chickadees, banana slugs, and tree frogs.

Stephanie's neighbors include lizards, burrowing owls, crabs, and cockroaches.